Rapunzel

Retold and illustrated by

Jutta Ash

ANDERSEN PRESS

ONCE upon a time, there lived a man and his wife and the one thing they lacked was a child. Now at the top of their house was a little room with a window which looked out over a beautiful walled garden. In it grew the loveliest flowers and the most luscious fruit and vegetables. But the wall around was high and what's more, the garden belonged to a witch!

One day, the wife noticed a bed planted with a special kind of fresh green lettuce known as rapunzel. How she longed to taste it! Very soon, she could think of nothing else. Day by day she grew paler and thinner, until she had dwindled into a shadow of herself, for no other food could tempt her, nothing at all.

THIS BOOK BELONGS TO:

_____

To the children in
St Thomas' Hospital

This paperback edition published in 2011 by Andersen Press Ltd.
First published in Great Britain in 1982 by Andersen Press Ltd.,
20 Vauxhall Bridge Road, London SW1V 2SA.
Published in Australia by Random House Australia Pty.,
Level 3, 100 Pacific Highway, North Sydney, NSW 2060.
Text and illustration copyright © Jutta Ash, 1982.
Originally colour separated in Switzerland by Photolitho AG, Zürich.
Additional scanning by SC (Sang Choy) International Pte Ltd, Singapore.
Printed and bound in China by C&C Offset Printing CO.,Ltd.

10   9   8   7   6   5   4   3   2   1

British Library Cataloguing in Publication Data available.
ISBN 978 1 84939 372 0
This book has been printed on acid-free paper

Her husband was alarmed to see her fading away. "Wife, wife,"
he said. "What is troubling you?"

"It's the rapunzel in that garden," she replied. "I shall die unless
I have some to eat."

"What's to be done?" thought the good man. "If she must
have it, she must, witch or no witch." So, that very evening, he
scrambled over the high wall, stealthily pulled up a bunch and
brought it back to his wife. Oh, she was overjoyed! She made it
into a salad and — crunch, crunch, how delicious! — in a minute
there wasn't a shred left. Next day, she craved for that green stuff
even more, there was nothing else she would eat.

What could the husband do? Again, he waited until dusk and climbed into the magic garden. He bent down to pick a quick handful of the rapunzel, but what a fright awaited him! There, standing over him, was the witch herself, wild with rage. "Thief!" she cried. "You'll regret it!" "Forgive me," begged the poor man, and he told her of his wife's great longing for the leaves. The witch grew calmer as she listened. "Very well," she said at last. "You may take as much as you need, but on one condition. As soon as your wife has a child, you must give that child to me. It will be well looked after, I promise you."

For Rapunzel had wonderful long golden hair which she often wore in thick plaits. Each time she heard the witch's call she would wind the plaits round the hook on the window ledge and let them fall all the way down to the ground. The witch would then seize hold and climb up until she reached the window.

Some years passed, and one day a young prince was riding through the wood. He heard the sound of sweet singing, followed the voice and found himself at the foot of a tall tower. But where was the door? Who was the singer? Whoever it was, the voice was so enchanting that the prince came day after day to listen.

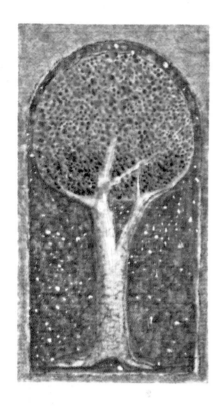  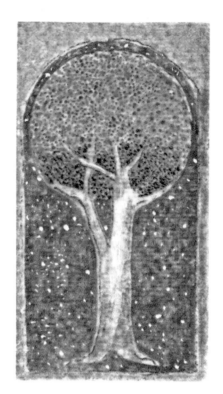

One evening, from his hiding place behind a tree, the prince
saw a strange woman emerge from the wood and stand at the
foot of the tower. There she called these words:

Rapunzel, Rapunzel,
Let down your golden hair!

At once a great length of golden hair slid to the ground, and the
woman hauled herself up to the window.
"Aha!" thought the prince. "A ladder for one is a ladder for
another!" So the next evening he too stood at the foot of the
tower and called up:

Rapunzel, Rapunzel,
Let down your golden hair!

Immediately the shining hair fell to his feet, and the prince
climbed up and up until he reached the window at the top.

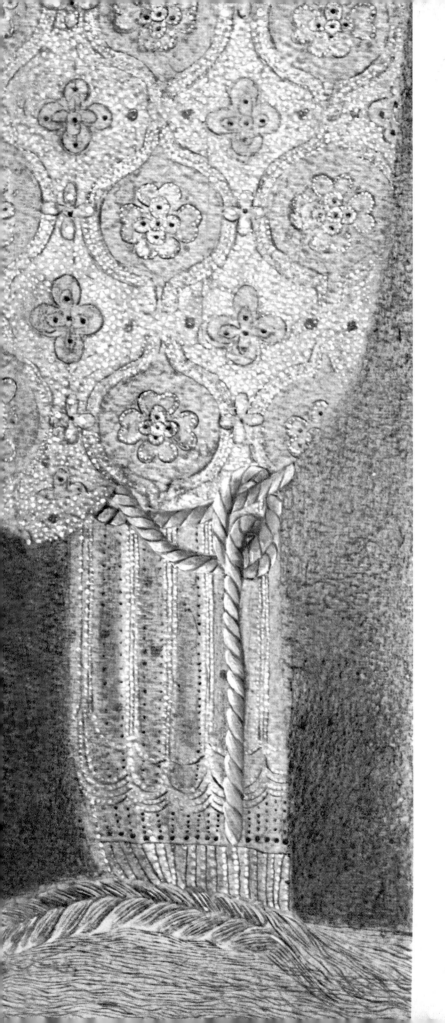

At first Rapunzel was alarmed when the prince appeared, for she had never seen anyone before but the witch. But he talked to her so kindly that she soon lost her fear. "Your singing brought me here," said the prince. "I listened so often." And he begged her to escape and be his wife.

"I would come gladly," said Rapunzel, "but how can it be done?"

At last they thought of a plan. Every night the prince would bring a skein of silk. Rapunzel would weave this into a ladder, and when it was long enough to reach the ground, she would climb down into freedom, and away they would ride together.

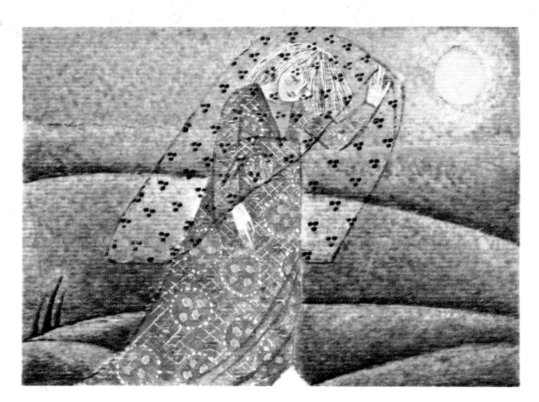

Each night the silken ladder grew longer and each day Rapunzel hid it well. But one day she made such a bad mistake! "Tell me, Mother," she said. "Why do you climb so slowly up to the window? The prince is here as quick as lightning." Oh – what had she said! The witch was in a frenzy.

"So you've had a visitor!" she hissed. "I thought I had kept you from the world, but you have deceived me. Well, there's an answer to that." She snatched up a pair of scissors, grasped the thick hair in her other hand, and – snip! snap! – the golden tresses fell and covered the floor. Then the witch dragged the poor girl off to a forest wilderness, and left her there to live on berries and nuts as well as she could.

Back in the tower the witch picked up the severed hair and wound it round the hook. She did not have to wait long. Far down below came the call:

Rapunzel, Rapunzel,
Let down your golden hair!

The golden hair came down and the prince climbed up — but imagine his horror when the window came into view! There he beheld not the lovely Rapunzel but the mocking face of the witch. "Ha!" she cried. "So you've come for my daughter! But you are too late — the bird has flown. You'll never see her again." She burst into peals of laughter — and the prince, maddened by the shock and despair, leapt from the window to the ground. Down . . . down . . .

He was not killed, for a great bush of thorns broke his fall.
But the thorns pierced his eyes and made him blind. Sadly
he wandered hither and thither, through the land, through
the forest, thinking only of the beautiful girl who should have
become his bride.

They made their joyful return to his kingdom,
where they all lived happily ever after.

Other books you might enjoy:

9781849390064

9781849393096

9781849392082

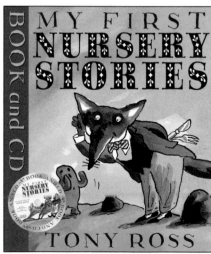

9781842709726

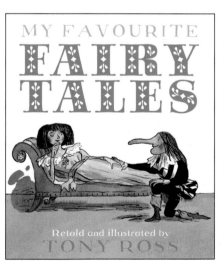

9781849392112